WELCOME TO
PASSPORT TO READING
A beginning reader's ticket to a brand-new world!

Every book in this program is designed to build read-along and read-alone skills, level by level, through engaging and enriching stories. As the reader turns each page, he or she will become more confident with new vocabulary, sight words, and comprehension.

These PASSPORT TO READING levels will help you choose the perfect book for every reader.

READING TOGETHER
Read short words in simple sentence structures together to begin a reader's journey.

READING OUT LOUD
Encourage developing readers to sound out words in more complex stories with simple vocabulary.

READING INDEPENDENTLY
Newly independent readers gain confidence reading more complex sentences with higher word counts.

READY TO READ MORE
Readers prepare for chapter books with fewer illustrations and longer paragraphs.

This book features sight words from the educator-supported Dolch Sight Words List. This encourages the reader to recognize commonly used vocabulary words, increasing reading speed and fluency.

For more information, please visit passporttoreadingbooks.com.

Enjoy the journey!

Little, Brown and Company

Hachette Book Group
237 Park Avenue, New York, NY 10017
Visit our website at lb-kids.com

Little, Brown and Company is a division of Hachette Book Group, Inc. The Little, Brown name and logo are trademarks of Hachette Book Group, Inc.

The publisher is not responsible for websites (or their content) that are not owned by the publisher.

First Edition: February 2014
Originally published in August 2008 as *A Fairy Tale* by Random House Children's Books, a division of Random House, Inc.

Library of Congress Control Number: 2013039048

ISBN 978-0-316-28327-4

10 9 8 7 6 5 4 3 2 1

CW

Printed in the United States of America

Passport to Reading titles are leveled by independent reviewers applying the standards developed by Irene Fountas and Gay Su Pinnell in *Matching Books to Readers: Using Leveled Books in Guided Reading*, Heinemann, 1999.

Meet Tinker Bell

By Apple Jordan

Illustrated by the Disney Storybook Art Team

LITTLE, BROWN AND COMPANY

New York • Boston

Attention, Disney Fairies fans!
Look for these words when you read
this book. Can you spot them all?

Silvermist

fireflies

owl

mouse

It is a big day for the fairies

who live in Pixie Hollow.

A new fairy is born.

Her name is Tinker Bell.

Queen Clarion tells Tinker Bell

she is born of laughter,

clothed in cheer,

and that happiness brought her here.

Each fairy has a talent.

What is Tinker Bell's talent?

The fairies give her light,

water, and flowers.

Nothing happens.

The fairies give Tinker Bell a hammer.

It glows.

Tinker Bell has found her talent!

She is a tinker fairy.

Tinkers fix things.

The other tinker fairies

welcome Tinker Bell.

Bobble and Clank show her
Pixie Hollow.

Then Tinker Bell meets Fairy Mary.

Fairy Mary is the head tinker.

"Being a tinker stinks,"
Tinker Bell tells Fairy Mary.
Tinker Bell wants to try
other talents.

Silvermist is a water fairy.

But Tink is not good with water.

She makes a splash.

Tink tries to be a light fairy.

The fireflies chase her away.

Tinker Bell tries to be an animal fairy.

She wants to help the baby owl.

But she scares the owl.

Tinker Bell keeps trying.

She tries to ride

Cheese the mouse.

Tinker Bell and Cheese

crash into the gate.

It opens.

All the Thistles run out.

The fairies are getting ready
for the spring season.
The Thistles run this way and that.
They run over the berries and seeds
for spring.

Tinker Bell made this mess.

Queen Clarion is upset.

How will they get ready

for spring now?

Tinker Bell has an idea.

She asks Bobble and Clank for help.

They make tools to make new things

for spring.

Tinker Bell saves spring
using her tinker talent.
All the fairies are happy.
The happiest fairy is
Queen Clarion.

Tinker Bell is happy.

She is a tinker fairy
and proud of it!